Dear Parent:
Your child's love of reading starts here!

Every child learns to read in a different way and at his or her own speed. Some go back and forth between reading levels and read favorite books again and again. Others read through each level in order. You can help your young reader improve and become more confident by encouraging his or her own interests and abilities. From books your child reads with you to the first books he or she reads alone, there are I Can Read Books for every stage of reading:

SHARED READING
Basic language, word repetition, and whimsical illustrations, ideal for sharing with your emergent reader

BEGINNING READING
Short sentences, familiar words, and simple concepts for children eager to read on their own

READING WITH HELP
Engaging stories, longer sentences, and language play for developing readers

READING ALONE
Complex plots, challenging vocabulary, and high-interest topics for the independent reader

ADVANCED READING
Short paragraphs, chapters, and exciting themes for the perfect bridge to chapter books

I Can Read Books have introduced children to the joy of reading since 1957. Featuring award-winning authors and illustrators and a fabulous cast of beloved characters, I Can Read Books set the standard for beginning readers.

A lifetime of discovery begins with the magical words "I Can Read!"

Visit www.icanread.com for information on enriching your child's reading experience.

To Dad and "Sink or Float"—
best bath game ever!

I Can Read Book® is a trademark of HarperCollins Publishers.
Balzer + Bray is an imprint of HarperCollins Publishers.

ISBN 978-0-06-236657-3 (pbk. bdg.) — ISBN 978-0-06-236658-0 (trade bdg.)

16 17 18 19 20   SCP   10 9 8 7 6 5 4 3 2 1
❖
First Edition

OTTER
Oh No, Bath Time!

By SAM GARTON

BALZER + BRAY

An Imprint of HarperCollinsPublishers

Teddy and I love
to play in the yard.

We do lots of fun things.

We play lots of games too.

Oh no, it looks like rain!

"Do not get muddy,"
says Otter Keeper.

Teddy and I love
to play in the rain.

We try to stay clean,
but it is very hard.

"You got very muddy,"
says Otter Keeper.
"Time for a bath."

12

Teddy and I do not like baths!
We have to hide.

We hide under the bed.

We hide in a box.

We even dress up.

Otter Keeper knows it is us.

Otter Keeper says
bath time is fun.
He says he will show us.

We are not so sure.

Teddy and I do not like baths!

First, Otter Keeper makes
lots of bubbles.

I love bubbles.

Next, Otter Keeper lets us
play with Duck.

We all make friends.

We also splash a lot.

Everything gets wet.

It is time to dry off.

Teddy wants another bath.

Otter Keeper says, "Not today."

Teddy and I are sad.

Then I have an idea.

Oh no, Teddy is
muddy again!

I must help him.

I tell Otter Keeper that
it's time for a bath.

Teddy and I love baths.